SASHA'S MATRIOSHKA DOLLS

Jana Dillon

Pictures by Deborah Nourse Lattimore

Farrar, Straus and Giroux • New York

Distributed in Canada by Douglas & McIntyre Ltd.
Color separations by Hong Kong Scanner Arts
Printed and bound in the United States of America by Phoenix Color Corporation
First edition, 2003
1 3 5 7 9 10 8 6 4 2

Library of Congress Cataloging-in-Publication Data
Dillon, Jana.
    Sasha's matrioshka dolls / Jana Dillon ; pictures by Deborah Nourse Lattimore.— 1st ed.
        p.   cm.
    Summary: Sasha's grandfather makes her a tiny wooden doll, but the mice are able to
carry it off, so he makes another slightly larger doll to hold the tiny one, and then
another, and another.
    ISBN 0-374-37387-6
    [1. Nesting dolls—Fiction.   2. Dolls—Fiction.   3. Russia—Fiction.]   I. Lattimore,
Deborah Nourse, ill.   II. Title.

PZ7.D5795 Tas 2002
[E]—dc21

                                                                                        00-39398

To my father, Frank Gerulskis, with love
—JD

To Beverly Reingold, with appreciation
—DNL

BOXER THE BOXMAKER AND SASHA, his granddaughter, lived and worked in their boxmaking shop on a busy street in old Moscow. Boxer built the boxes. Sasha painted them.

It took Boxer a long time to make each box. It didn't take Sasha long to paint swirling, bursting, blooming sprays of flowers on them. So each day Sasha had hours to play with her one doll, a rag doll, in the sunny shop window.

"You are so slow, Grandfather Boxer," she said, teasing. "Look at me, *playing*. My work is finished."

"Slow, she says." Boxer snorted, but he couldn't help smiling.

One morning Sasha awoke to find her rag doll in shreds on the floor. The mice had chewed it apart and run off with the stuffing for their beds.

"My doll!" Sasha wailed. "It's ruined! Grandfather Boxer, come quick!"

Boxer shook his fist at the walls where the mice lived. "You thieving mice!"

"Now I have no doll," said Sasha. Tears filled her eyes.

"Oh, my Sasha," said Boxer. "You know I can't sew. I can't make you a new rag doll."

"No doll?" Sasha tried not to burst into sobs.

"Wait! Sasha, I can carve!" said Boxer. "Come into my workshop. I'll carve you a doll—a thumbling doll—from a scrap of wood."

"Can you really?" Sasha asked.

"Am I not the best woodworker in Moscow?" asked Boxer.

"We'll see," said Sasha.

"Ha!" said Boxer. "When you can tease, I know you are happy again."

Boxer whittled the wood into a head and body. "Now you paint it, Sasha," he said. "See what you can do."

Sasha took out her finest sable brush and went to work. The only sounds that could be heard in the shop were the *risp-rasp* of Boxer's sandpaper, the *slip-slap* of Sasha's paints, and the *scritch-scratch* of the mice behind the walls. Just once were they interrupted by the greetings of a customer.

"Look, Grandfather Boxer!" Sasha called with delight. "I have painted a matrioshka, a little mother."

"A little mother," whispered Boxer with tears in his eyes. "Like your little mother, my daughter, once was. And like her little mother, my wife. Someday, Sasha, you too will be a little mother." Boxer sighed. "Well, now you have a doll again, my dear."

"I love her," said Sasha. "I love *you*, Grandfather. Thank you for making her."

Boxer was so pleased by her joy and gratitude that he added, "I will make you a perfect box of the same shape to store her in. After all, I am a boxmaker."

"I will paint the box just the way I painted the matrioshka, and I will have two dolls," said Sasha, dancing about, "one to talk to the other."

At bedtime Sasha kissed her matrioshka dolls good night. She carefully nestled the thumbling doll inside the other. She left them on the work-table and went to bed.

But the next morning the matrioshkas were gone. "Grandfather, where could they be?" cried Sasha.

"Who would steal a little girl's dolls?" thundered Boxer. "This is outrageous!"

Sasha began to search for clues under the tables and behind the curtains. Boxer tore through the piles of wood curls, scattering them like a windstorm.

"Strange," said Sasha, stopping suddenly. "Listen to that rolling sound behind the wallboards. Do you think . . . ?"

Boxer threw himself down on his hands and knees and peered fiercely into the mousehole. "Aha! You rascals!" he roared. "How dare you steal my granddaughter's dolls!"

The mice scattered. Boxer reached in and rescued the matrioshkas.

"Your dolls are safe," said Boxer. "Don't worry, Sasha, I'll make you a third matrioshka box. Together, the dolls will be too large and heavy for the mice to move. We'll have no more trouble from those heartless little thieves."

Not one customer came by that morning, so Sasha soon had another matrioshka doll to paint. As she finished, the church bells in the Kremlin rang out the noon hour.

Sasha and Boxer sat down in the kitchen to a fragrant meal of sweet beet soup, black bread, and cheese.

"No customers," said Boxer with a sigh. "Business is so slow."

"Grandfather!" shrieked Sasha. "Look!"

A huge rat raced across the kitchen floor. The matrioshkas were between his teeth.

"The broom!" yelled Boxer. He swung it at the thief.

The rat leaped high and squealed in anger, and the matrioshkas fell to the floor. The rat scurried behind the wall.

"Once again I have saved your little doll," said Boxer, out of breath. "But now I must make another box for her, one that is too big for rats."

Sasha looked pleased. "That will make four dolls."

"Four!" Boxer's voice boomed. "I am beginning to believe that I will be making bigger and bigger matrioshka boxes for the rest of my life."

Boxer was silent for a moment until a thought struck him. "Maybe a cat will solve our problem."

"Oh, yes," said Sasha. "I've always wanted a cat."

Lady Mouser was an excellent cat. She chased everything: sunbeams, dust motes, shadows . . .

Lady Mouser watched Sasha turn the fourth nesting doll this way and that as she brushed on the paint. *Meow,* the cat called sweetly. *Meow.*

When the new doll was dry, Sasha placed the others inside her and left them on the worktable.

Meow.

Bang! Crash! Slam! Boxer and Sasha ran from the kitchen into the shop to find Lady Mouser batting and chasing the matrioshkas across the floor.

Meow! Lady Mouser cried as she leaped and wrestled and rolled over the spinning matrioshkas.

"Drop those dolls, you foolish cat!" shouted Boxer.

"The matrioshkas need another box to make them heavier still," said Boxer, throwing up his hands in exasperation. "I can see it now. I will be making a new matrioshka every day for the rest of my life. Soon the dolls will not fit inside the house. They will be as big as a cathedral! I will have to hire men with ladders to work on each new one."

"But think of all the dolls I'll have," said Sasha with a smile.

Boxer snorted and rolled his eyes, amused in spite of himself.

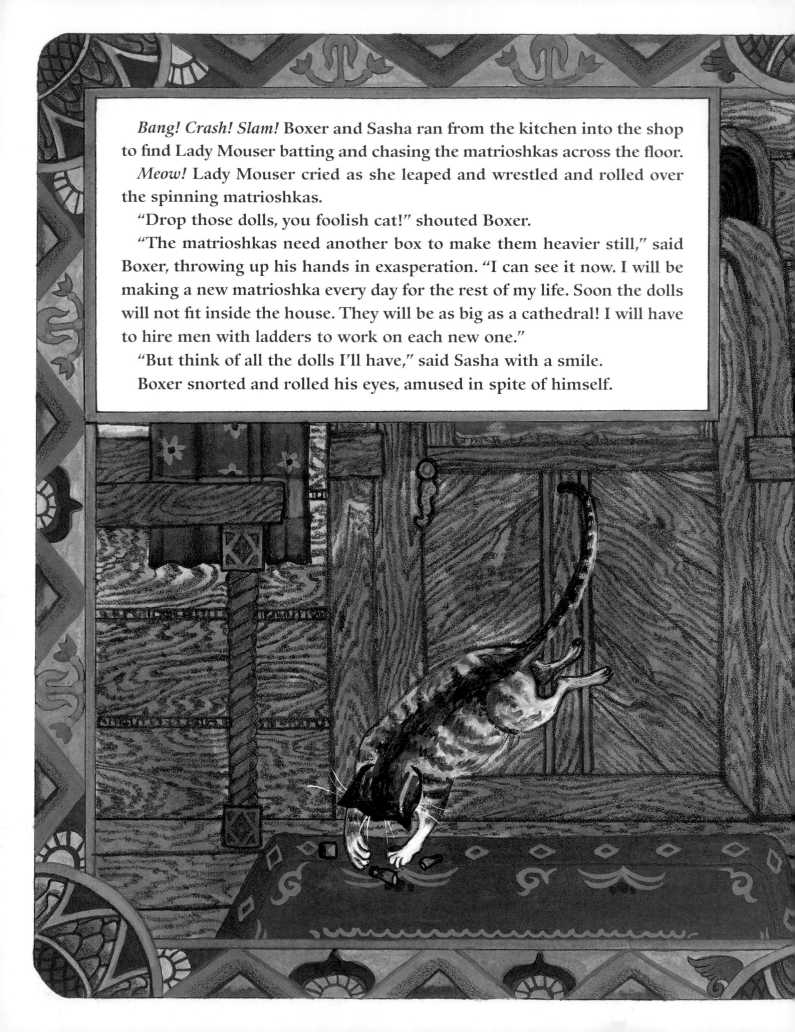

That night they carefully placed the matrioshkas on the kitchen table, and kept an eye on the dolls from their beds by the stove.

"Who would have imagined that one little thumbling doll would need so many boxes to keep her safe?" Boxer murmured as he fell asleep.

Sasha wondered about that for a while. "Who would have imagined," she whispered to Lady Mouser, "that one little gift, a tiny doll, would grow so? Now I have five dolls, each bigger than the last."

The next day Sasha was busy painting flowers on boxes while Boxer built new ones. "I hope these boxes attract customers," said Boxer.

They heard a faint rumbling sound. It grew louder and louder.

"Is that thunder?" asked Sasha.

"It's the Tsar's cavalry!" said Boxer. "Hold on to the boxes! To the paints! Here they come!"

The windowpanes rattled and the ground shook as the soldiers galloped past on their powerful horses.

The boxes and the paints were safe, but the matrioshkas quaked and bobbled on the bouncing table. They toppled over. Grandfather and Sasha watched them roll across the floor, round and round and round.

"I can see I must make another matrioshka box," said Boxer with a loud, dramatic sigh.

"I'm afraid only *one* won't do," said Sasha, trying not to smile. "Not with the heavy hoofbeats of the cavalry shaking things so."

"I see," said Boxer slowly. "Then I must make *two* matrioshka boxes."

Boxer looked at Sasha. He tried to look upset.

Sasha looked at Boxer. She tried to look serious.

They burst out laughing.

When Sasha finished painting, she had seven matrioshka dolls. Seven dolls were enough.

Sasha played with her dolls in the sunny shop window. People walking past expected to see the floppy old rag doll in her hands. But no! Here were seven wooden matrioshkas, six fitting inside another. They had never seen such dolls.

More and more people gathered at the window to watch Sasha play. They discussed the dolls: Were all the dolls mothers? Or was one the mother and the rest her married daughters? Were they seven sisters? Were they generations—mother, grandmother, great-grandmother . . . ?

Finally people came into the shop to find out.

"Sasha says they are all little mothers," said Boxer. "Maybe they are neighbors, maybe sisters, she hasn't told me."

"I want to order a set of seven."

"Me too."

"And I."

Boxer had never known such prosperity. Orders for dolls poured in day after day, week after week, month after month.

"You were right, Grandfather Boxer," Sasha said. "You will be making matrioshkas every day, doll after doll after doll, for the rest of your life."

Bowing, Boxer said, "And for that I must give thanks where thanks are due. Thank you, mice. Thank you, rat. Thank you, cat. Thank you, horses." He held Sasha's hand and kissed it. "And thank you, dear Sasha, for needing not one but seven dolls."

"Oh, no, no," said Sasha, taking both of Boxer's hands in her own. "Thank you, Grandfather Boxer. Each doll was a gift of love."

She bowed in turn, kissed him, and ran off to her place in the sunny window to play with her seven matrioshkas.

AUTHOR'S NOTE

Russian nesting dolls, commonly called matrioshkas, first appeared in Moscow in the late nineteenth century. They are believed to have been carved in the Children's Education workshop at Abramtsevo, the estate owned by the Mamontov family, industrialists and art collectors interested in promoting a distinctly Russian cultural identity. Although nesting boxes and similar objects dating back hundreds of years have been discovered in China and Japan, and nesting dolls are produced in several countries today, the Russian matrioshkas are the best known.

The matrioshka varies according to the culture of the geographic region where the artisans live. Sasha's "little mothers" are taken from the style of Polkholvsky Maidan, a village south of Moscow whose craftsmen celebrate the family values of the country peasants.